LOOK AT THE

BIRDS

WRITTEN AND ILLUSTRATED BY
Lisa Anne Tindal

ISBN 978-1-63630-433-5 (Paperback)
ISBN 978-1-63630-434-2 (Hardcover)
ISBN 978-1-63630-435-9 (Digital)

Covenant Books, Inc.
11661 Hwy 707
Murrells Inlet, SC 29576
www.covenantbooks.com

DEDICATION

To my daughter, Heather, the mother of sweet Elizabeth Lettie and to my mother in heaven "Grandma Bette" who inspired the promise I'd be keeping when God gave me a new name, "Grandma". To Greg and to Austin who encourage me in different ways to be brave, to be victorious. To my grandmother, a lover of every bird and to my precious Aunt "Boo" who laid a foundation of prayer and patience and continues to guide me with her wisdom. Most of all, to my heavenly Father who transformed my life through Jesus and who gave me the verse I call life, "In quietness and confidence is your strength." Isaiah 30:15 NLT

"Look at the birds," said Grandma to baby. "Look at the birds!"

A tiny bluebird is hop-hopping in the big field.

"Look at the birds," said Grandma to baby.
"Look at the birds."

A little brown sparrow has landed on the porch.

"Look at the birds," said Grandma to baby. "Look at the birds."

A strong hawk is circling up high toward heaven.

"Look at the birds," said Grandma to baby. "Look at the birds!"

A plump robin is playing in the yellow flowers.

"Look at the birds," said Grandma to baby.
"Look at the birds."

A black crow is flying to join its good friend.

"Look at the birds," said Grandma to baby. "Look at the birds!"

A bright cardinal is crossing quickly in front of our path.

"Look at the birds," said Grandma to baby.
"Look at the birds."

A finch is flying by your very own
window on the way to its nest.

"Look at the birds," said Grandma to baby.
"Look at the birds and remember
you are loved so much more."

"Look at the birds," said Grandma to baby.
"Look at the birds!"

Look at the birds of the air: they neither
sow nor reap nor gather into barns, and your
heavenly Father feeds them. Are you not of
more value than they? (Matthew 6:26 ESV)

"Look at the birds," said Jesus to Grandma,
"look at the ways you are loved."

"Look at the birds," said Grandma to baby again.

Look at the birds and remember not to worry,
for our Father in heaven who made all the babies,
birds, and grandmas will always love you too.

ABOUT THE AUTHOR

Lisa Anne Tindal retired from Child Welfare and Non-Profit leadership to begin a beautiful new career, helping care for her granddaughter. With the transition came a renewed love of art and writing, and a connectedness with God through nature as well as through the eyes of a baby. The experience of being a grandmother also brought personal challenges, a role vastly different than lifelong professions, which led to a greater understanding of trusting God. Walking and looking at the birds, the sky, trees, and simply God's earth is a daily practice Lisa Anne calls "noticing God."

Lisa Anne is married, has a daughter who teaches first grade, a son who is an accountant, and a stepson who is an engineer. God has greatly blessed their family with four grandchildren. Lisa Anne blogs about redemption and a faith that continues to increase as she continues to believe. Lisa Anne has contributed to Fathom Magazine as an artist and writer and contributed to a book on motherhood, "I Heart Mom." Her writing can be found at https://www.quietconfidence-artandword.blog and her art can be viewed at https://www.lisaannetindal.com.